# LITTLE GOLDEN BOOK® CLASSICS
## CLASSICS
### *Featuring the art of*
### Garth Williams

## *Three Best-Loved Tales*

### MY FIRST COUNTING BOOK
**By Lilian Moore**

### THE KITTEN WHO THOUGHT
### HE WAS A MOUSE
**By Miriam Norton**

### HOME FOR A BUNNY
**By Margaret Wise Brown**

A GOLDEN BOOK • NEW YORK
Western Publishing Company, Inc., Racine, Wisconsin 53404

# MY FIRST COUNTING BOOK

By Lilian Moore

**1**

One little puppy,
A roly-poly puppy, alone as he can be.
"Isn't there a boy or girl
Who wants to play with me?"

Two little woolly lambs
Looking for their mother.
Two little woolly lambs,
A sister and a brother.

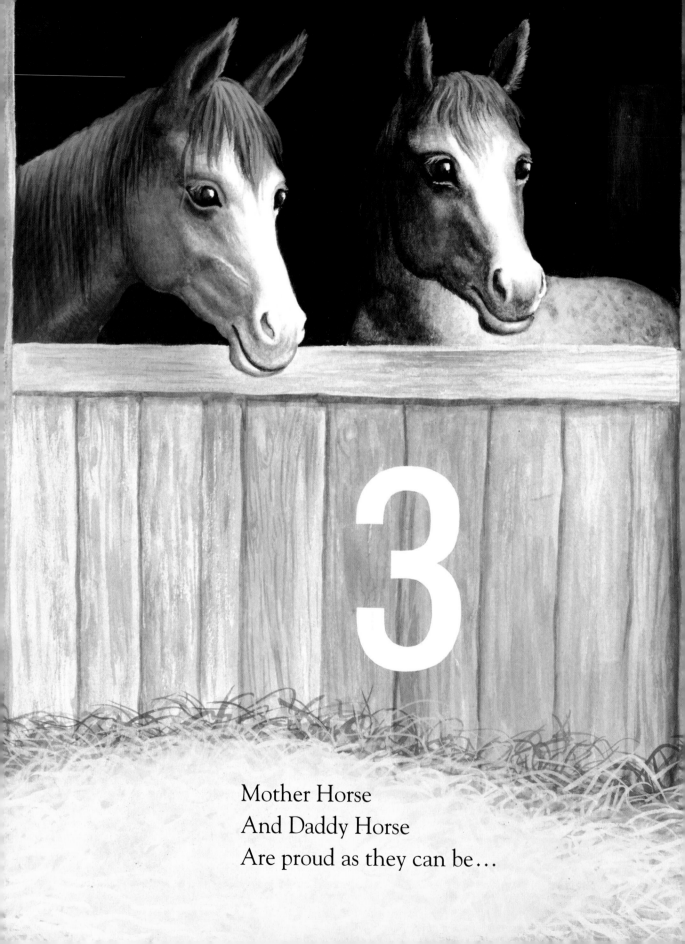

Mother Horse
And Daddy Horse
Are proud as they can be...

Because they have a baby horse,
And Baby Horse makes three.

Four furry, purry kittens
Look alike because

4

Each furry, purry kitten
Has four white paws.

5

Bunny finds five cabbages—
One, two, three, four, five—
Near the garden wall.
Bunny sniffs five cabbages,
And Bunny wants them all.

One, two, three,
Four, five, six.
First they were eggs...

Now they are chicks!

Waddle, waddle, waddle,
The baby ducklings go,
Waddling after Mother Duck,
Seven in a row.

7

Swish, swish,
Eight fish
Swimming in the brook…

Swish, swish,
Wise fish,
Swimming past the hook.

8

Hurry and count them
As they fly.
You will see nine geese,
And so will I!

How many nuts did you find,
Little Squirrel,
Looking high and low?
Chitter, chatter,
What's the matter?
Don't you know?
Little Squirrel, I'll tell you, then.
Little Squirrel, you found ten.

10

# THE KITTEN
# WHO THOUGHT
# HE WAS A MOUSE

By Miriam Norton

There were five Miggses: Mother and Father
Miggs and Lester and two sisters.

They had, as field mice usually do, an outdoor nest for summer in an empty lot and an indoor nest for winter in a nearby house.

They were very surprised one summer day to find
a strange bundle in their nest, a small gray-and-black
bundle of fur and ears and legs, with eyes not yet
open. They knew by its mewing that the bundle
must be a kitten, a lost kitten with no family and
no name.

"Poor kitty," said the sisters.
"Let him stay with us," said Lester.
"But a cat!" said Mother Miggs.

"Why not?" said Father Miggs.

"We can bring him up to be a good mouse. He need never find out he is really a cat. You'll see—he'll be a good thing for this family."

"Let's call him Mickey," said Lester.

And that's how Mickey Miggs found his new family and a name.

After his eyes opened he began to grow up just as mice do, eating all kinds of seeds and bugs and drinking from puddles and sleeping in a cozy pile of brother and sister mice.

Father Miggs showed him his first tomcat—at a safe distance—and warned him to "keep away from all cats and dogs and people."

Mickey saw his first mousetrap—"The most dangerous thing of all," said Mother Miggs—when they moved to the indoor nest that fall.

He was too clumsy to steal bait from traps himself, so Lester and the sisters had to share with him what they stole.

But Mickey was useful in fooling the household cat, Hazel. He practiced up on meowing, for usually, of course, he squeaked, and became clever at what he thought was imitating a cat.

He would hide in a dark corner and then, "Meow! Meow!" he'd cry. Hazel would poke around, leaving the pantry shelves unguarded while she looked for the other cat. That gave Lester and his sisters a chance to make a raid on the leftovers.

Poor Hazel! She knew she heard, even smelled, another cat, and sometimes saw cat's eyes shining in a corner. But no cat ever came out to meet her.

How could she know that Mickey didn't know he was a cat at all and that he feared Hazel as much as the mousiest mouse would!

And so Mickey Miggs grew, becoming a better mouse all the time and enjoying his life. He loved cheese, bacon, and cake crumbs. He got especially good at smelling out potato skins and led the sisters and Lester straight to them every time.

"A wholesome and uncatlike food," said Mother Miggs to Father Miggs approvingly. "Mickey is doing well." And Father Miggs said to Mother Miggs, "I told you so!"

Then one day, coming from a nap in the wastepaper basket, Mickey met the children of the house, Peggy and Paul.

"*Ee-eeeeeek!*" Mickey squeaked in terror. He dashed along the walls of the room looking for his mousehole.

"It's a kitten!" cried Peggy as Mickey squeezed through the hole.

"But it acts like a mouse," said Paul.

The children could not understand why the

kitten had been so mouselike, but they decided to try to make friends with him.

That night, as Mickey came out of his hole, he nearly tripped over something lying right there in front of him. He sniffed at it. It was a dish and in the dish was something to drink.

"What is it?" asked Mickey. Lester didn't know, but timidly tried a little. "No good," he said, shaking his whiskers.

Mickey tried it, tried some more, then some more and some more and more and more—until it was all gone.

"Mmmmmmmmmmm!" he said. "What wonderful stuff."

"It's probably poison and you'll get sick," said Lester disgustedly. But it wasn't poison and Mickey had a lovely feeling in his stomach from drinking it. It was milk, of course. And every night that week Mickey found a saucer of milk outside that same hole. He lapped up every drop.

"He drank it, he drank it!" cried Peggy and Paul happily each morning. They began to set out a saucerful in the daytime, too.

At first Mickey would drink the milk only when he was sure Peggy and Paul were nowhere around. Soon he grew bolder and began to trust them in the room with him.

And soon he began to let them come nearer and nearer and nearer still.

Then one day he found himself scooped up and held in Peggy's arms. He didn't feel scared. He felt fine. And he felt a queer noise rumble up his back and all through him. It was Mickey's first purr.

Peggy and Paul took Mickey to a shiny glass on
the wall and held him close in front of it. Mickey,
who had never seen a mirror, saw a cat staring at
him there, a cat in Paul's arms where he thought *he*
was. He began to cry, and his cry instead of being a
squeak was a mewing wail.

Finally Mickey began to understand that he was not a mouse like Lester and his sisters, but a cat like Hazel.

He stayed with Peggy and Paul that night, trying not to be afraid of his own cat-self. He still didn't quite believe it all, however, and next morning he crept back through his old hole straight to Mother Miggs.

"Am I really a cat?" he cried.

"Yes," said Mother Miggs sadly. And she told him the whole story of how he was adopted and brought up as a mouse. "We loved you and wanted you to love us," she explained. "It was the only safe and fair way to bring you up."

After talking with Mother Miggs, Mickey decided to be a cat in all ways. He now lives with Peggy and Paul, who also love him, and who can give him lots of good milk and who aren't afraid of his purr or his meow.

Mickey can't really forget his upbringing, however. He takes an old rubber mouse of Peggy's to bed with him.

He often visits the Miggses in the indoor nest, where he nibbles cheese tidbits and squeaks about old times.

And of course he sees to it that Hazel no longer prowls in the pantry at night.

"Oh, I'm so fat and stuffed from eating so much in Hazel's pantry," Father Miggs often says happily to Mother Miggs. "I always said our Mickey would be a good thing for the family—and he is!"

# HOME
# FOR A BUNNY

By Margaret Wise Brown

"Spring, Spring, Spring!"
sang the frog.
"Spring!"
said the groundhog.

"Spring, Spring, Spring!" sang the robin.
It was Spring.
The leaves burst out.
The flowers burst out.
And robins burst out of their eggs.
It was Spring.

In the Spring a bunny
came down the road.
    He was going to find
a home of his own.
    A home for a bunny,
    A home of his own,
    Under a rock,
    Under a stone,
    Under a log,
    Or under the ground.
    Where would a bunny find a home?

"Where is your home?"
he asked the robin.

"Here, here, here,"
sang the robin.
"Here in this nest is my home."

"Here, here, here,"
sang the little robins
who were about to fall out of the nest.
"Here is our home."

"Not for me," said the bunny.
"I would fall out of a nest.
I would fall on the ground."

So he went on
looking for a home.
"Where is your home?"
he asked the frog.

"Wog, wog, wog,"
sang the frog.
"Wog, wog, wog,
Under the water,
Down in the bog."
"Not for me,"
said the bunny.
"Under the water,
I would drown in a bog."

So he went on
looking for a home.
"Where do you live?"
he asked the groundhog.
"In a log," said the groundhog.
"Can I come in?" said the bunny.
"No, you can't come in my log,"
said the groundhog.

So the bunny went down the road.
　　Down the road
and down the road he went.
　　He was going to find
a home of his own.
　　A home for a bunny,
　　A home of his own,
　　Under a rock
　　Or a log
　　Or a stone.
　　Where would a bunny find a home?

Down the road
and down the road
and down the road
he went, until—

He met a bunny.
"Where is your home?"
he asked the bunny.

"Here," said the bunny.
"Here is my home.
Under this rock,
Under this stone,
Down under the ground,
Here is my home."

"Can I come in?"
said the bunny.
"Yes," said the bunny.
And so he did.

And that was his home.

# *About* Garth Williams

During his forty year career, Garth Williams has illustrated a number of children's books that are already considered classics. He brought to life such beloved animal characters as Wilbur the Pig of E. B. White's *Charlotte's Web* and Stuart Little, White's famous mouse, from the book of the same name, both published by Harper Brothers.

It was at Golden Books that Williams further demonstrated his remarkable ability to individualize animal characters and imbue them with human emotions. When asked how he accomplished this, the artist explained, "I start with the real animal, working over and over until I can get the effect of human qualities and expressions and poses. I redesign the animals, as it were."

Williams was born in 1912 in New York City. His parents were both artists. When he was eighteen, he began to study painting in London at the Westminster Art School and also at the Royal College of Art. In 1936 he was awarded the British Prix de Rome for sculpture. When World War II began in England, he served in the British Red Cross until he was injured in the London Blitz.

Williams returned to New York and landed a job at the *New Yorker* magazine in 1941. It was there that E. B. White asked him to illustrate *Stuart Little*. The experience was so successful that the artist concentrated on children's book illustration from then on.

Over the years, several of Garth Williams' books were recognized as American Library Association Notable Books. Among these was one of the Laura Ingalls Wilder "Little House" books. Williams devoted many years to illustrating a new edition of the series which was published in 1953 by Harper.

Garth Williams's long association with Golden Books began when he was asked to illustrate Dorothy Kunhardt's Tiny Golden Library, published in 1949. Dorothy Kunhardt was the author and illustrator of Golden's famous *Pat the Bunny* book.

In subsequent years, the artist collaborated with the well-known author Margaret Wise Brown on a number of excellent Little Golden Books. One of the best of these, *Home for a Bunny,* is included in this volume.